BILLY WANTS IT ALL

BILLY GROWING UP SERIES: VALUE OF MONEY

James Minter

Helen Rushworth - Illustrator

www.billygrowingup.com

MINTER PUBLISHING LIMITED

Minter Publishing Limited (MPL)
4 Lauradale, Bracknell RG12 7DT

Paperback ISBN: 978-1-910727-24-9
Hardback ISBN: 978-1-910727-26-3
eBook ISBN: 978-1-910727-25-6

Illustrations copyright © Helen Rushworth

Printed and bound in Great Britain by Ingram Spark,
Milton Keynes

>>>>>
DEDICATED to those who think money grows on
tress – think again.
<<<<<

This book belongs to

....

I give it

stars

1

AT THE
SUPERMARKET

"Oh, Mum, do I have to?" Billy slumped down in the back seat of the car and clicked the seatbelt into place. "It's not fair! Why do I always have to go to the supermarket?" He stared hard at the back of his mum's head as she drove. He hoped she might turn into an alien or something. *Anything* rather than go shopping.

"Funny, you didn't say that when we went to London looking for that new skateboard shop." His mum watched him in the rear-view mirror.

Billy noticed and snarled back at her, "Yeah, well ... that's different."

"I'll tell you what, you stop eating, or wearing clothes, or going to the toilet, or having a shower, or cleaning your teeth, or any of the other things you do, like having clean sheets on your bed, shoes on your feet, and Jacko as a pet, then you won't need to come shopping. How does that sound?"

"Muuum, be serious. All I'm saying is why do I have to go shopping?" Billy gazed out of the car window; they passed the park. "Look! See, it's Tom, Ant, and Khalid." He tapped his finger hard against the glass, trying to get her attention. "Please, Mum, stop and let me out."

"I know that Lindy takes Ant and Max when she goes shopping, so why shouldn't you come with me?" Billy's mum slowed the car as they approached a pedestrian crossing. The lights had turned red. By chance, Lindy and Max stood on the crossing.

"See!" Billy screeched, "Ant's not with them." He crossed his arms over his chest and jabbed his fists deep into his armpits while pushing his chin forward.

"You can sulk all you like, but you're help me with the shopping."

Billy took a trolley and scooted across the car park, following his mum into the supermarket. As they wandered up and down each aisle, working their way through a long list of items, every now and then, Billy's hand would shoot out. He waited until his mum got distracted reading a label or trying to work out how many ounces in a gram, and then he would grab a packet of sweets or biscuits or shower gel in a Spiderman-shaped bottle, or anything else that took his fancy.

"No, Billy! How many more times?" His mum reached into the trolley and put each item back, placing them randomly on shelves that contained something totally unrelated but which they happened to be passing at the time. "You know money doesn't grow on trees." His mum narrowed her eyes and glared at him. "And anyway, too much sugar is bad for you."

"Yeah, but what about the Spiderman shower gel? You want me to be nice and clean, don't you?"

"Did you see the price of it compared to the supermarket's brand? It's twice as much." His mum held his gaze.

"I suppose so." Billy dropped his head. As he did, he spotted one of those dental chew dog bones. "What about this?" Billy grabbed the packet. "If you get this for Jacko, you won't have to pay for a dog dentist." Proud, he waved the bone in his mum's face.

"Now, that makes sense. Investing in this dog chew today could mean we'll save on vet bills in the future." She took the packet from Billy and dropped it into the trolley.

Billy screwed up his eyes and creased his brow, "In whating?"

"Investing. ... It's when you make money work for you." His mum reached into the trolley and took up the chew bone again. "See here; the price is four pounds and eighty pence." She held it out for Billy to see. "But the last time we got Jacko's teeth cleaned by the vet it cost over two hundred and seventy pounds."

"Crikey, that's nearly the cost of two skateboards. The one I want is only one hundred and forty pounds." Billy took the bone back. "Does that mean if we buy this, you can buy me my skateboard with the money saved?" He tilted his head to one side and made a cheesy grin. "Please," he added, for good measure.

His mum pretended not to hear as she loaded more items into the trolley. "Pick up that sack of potatoes for me, please, and then we're finished."

Billy squatted and lifted the sack. He let out a grunt as he strained. "Well?" he asked again.

His mum still didn't answer. "A growing boy like you should be able to lift that."

Billy staggered, lifting the sack high enough to push it over the side of the trolley. It dropped onto all the other shopping.

"Careful, or you'll crush everything." Billy's mum manoeuvred the sack to one side. "Right, let's go and pay."

The car boot shut with a loud thud. "Okay, good job. Time to get this lot home." Billy's mum slipped into the driver's seat.

On the far side of the car park, Billy saw some teenagers practicing with their skateboards.

"Look, Mum, see that boy there?" Billy pushed his arm between the car's front seats and pointed, "The one in the blue jacket. He's got the board I want—an Element Nyjah Weaver. I saw it in the *Boards and Bikes* catalogue."

"But you've got a skateboard, the one you bought from Dan Prescott with your birthday money. What's wrong with that?" Billy's mum drove on, leaving Billy hanging over the back seat and watching his dream board disappear into the distance.

"It's okay, but I'm getting really good. Even Stu says so."

"Stu … Stewart Dunderdale? I told you to keep away from him." Billy's mum frowned.

Billy didn't see, as he still sat looking out of the back window, but he heard his mum's disapproval.

"Yeah, but he reckons I ought to go in for the under-fifteens competition."

"But you're only ten." His mum sounded hesitant, "Are you sure he said fifteen?"

"Yeah, 'cos that's how good I am." Billy's smile couldn't have been wider as he thought about what Stu had said. "So, can I?"

"How's your friend Ant getting on? Is he as good as you?" Billy's mum stopped the car outside their house.

"He's learning slowly, but he's nervous after breaking his arm where he smashed into that tree on his bike."

"I'm sure he is. Are you helping him to improve his skateboarding?"

"Not really; I let him use my board sometimes, but he can't even drop or pump or do a kick turn." Billy sounded very matter of fact, but his mum didn't have a clue as to what he was talking about.

"Oh, that's a shame. Maybe you can teach him." His mum rubbed her chin while she thought. "You say Stu says you're good enough to go in for the under-fifteens competition. Does that mean there are lots of children who aren't that good compared to you?"

"I guess so." Billy had the sack of potatoes over his shoulder as he strode up the garden path. "Where do you want these?"

"What about giving lessons? If you're that good, you can offer to teach other children and charge them. Then your skateboard becomes an investment, as you can earn money from it and put it toward that elephant hinge thingy board you want."

"Oh, Mum, it's called an Element Nyjah Weaver."

2

TABLET COMPUTERS FOR ALL

"Have you seen this?" Ant, Billy's best friend, pulled a folded scrap of paper from his schoolbag. "It's from our school's parent-teacher group or whatever they're called." Ant stopped walking and pulled at Billy's arm. "Oi."

"What?" Billy stopped also. "What is it?"

"This." Ant waved the paper in his face. "Have you seen it? It's so exciting." Ant ran in a circle around Billy.

"Yeah, I got one, I think. What's it about?" Billy snatched the paper from Ant and read it aloud. "Wow! Tablet computers for all of year five and six students. Awesome!" Billy high-fived Ant. "That's mega."

"Yeah, but it says the PTA are looking to all parents to help with fund raising or for a donation." Ant's smile turned upside down. "I'm not sure Mum and Dad can afford it. Don't they cost hundreds of pounds?"

"About five hundred, I think." Billy's face dropped too when he realised the price.

"We can't end up the only ones in class without one." Ant kicked at a stone as they continued their walk toward the bike sheds. "I don't think Tom's mum will have the money. She has three kids—Katie, who's in the same class as my sister Max, and then Tom, and of course, stinker Eddy, who's at secondary school. He doesn't deserve one."

The excitement over the tablets slipped away. Both boys looked glum as they unlocked their bikes before pulling them from the racks.

Ant turned to Billy. "Anyway, what were you thinking about?"

"When?"

"Just now, in the playground. When I tried to show you that bit of paper, you were like a zombie." Ant pushed on his bike's pedal and moved off.

"I thought about what my mum said to me when we went to the supermarket." Billy pulled alongside Ant.

"I might have some superpowers, but mind reading isn't one of them. What did your mum say?" Ant stared at Billy.

"Um … oh, yeah … no… I mean, mum told me about investing."

Ant thought for a bit. "Is that like getting dressed, like climbing into your trousers? You know, when you put on a vest, do you get into your vest? Get it, in … vest … ing."

"What are you going on about now? It's got nothing to do with getting dressed or trousers; it's about money." Billy looked at Ant as if he had two heads. "You know Stu says I'm a natural at skateboarding and should go into the—"

"Yeah, yeah ... under-fifteens competition. How many more times?"

"Well, I need an Element Nyjah Weaver board if I've a chance at winning, but they cost a hundred and forty pounds. So, Mum came up with the idea of me using the board I bought from Dan and giving lessons to other kids. That'll give me money, which I can save toward my new board. That's investing."

"Do you think anyone will pay for lessons?" Ant didn't sound too sure.

"I dunno until I try."

The boys arrived outside Ant's garden gate. Ant's bike brakes let out a piercing scream when he stopped.

"You need to get those sorted," Billy suggested.

"Suppose so. See ya." Ant disappeared around the back of his house; Billy rode on to his grandad's. He lived only two houses away from Ant. Billy always went there after school to wait for one of his parents to get back from work.

"Woof, woof." Jacko, Billy's bestest dog, had heard Billy open Grandad's back door. Before Billy had a chance to get through it, the dog licked at his hand and twisted and turned his body to get Billy to stroke and fuss over him. Billy and Jacko had become inseparable.

"I thought it was you." Grandad hobbled into his kitchen, "These knees of mine are giving me gyp. I can hardly walk." Grandad sat down slowly, using his hands to help him into the chair. "Help your old grandad and put the kettle on, please?"

Billy edged his way over to the sink.

"Can I have a biscuit?" Billy rubbed Jacko's tummy, "Please, Grandad. ... Hello, boy; have you missed me?" Billy pushed past the dog and dropped his high-vis jacket, helmet, and schoolbag in a heap on the floor. "Come on, boy ... up." Billy patted his chest, and Jacko stood on his back legs, resting his front paws on Billy's shoulder.

"Well, he seems excited to see you." Grandad placed a mug of tea alongside a single custard cream biscuit—Billy's favourites.

"Okay, Jacks, that's enough." Billy helped the dog down, "I need to talk to Grandad."

"Oh, that sounds important." Grandad dunked his digestive biscuit into his tea.

"It's about what Mum said to me, about investing." Billy split his biscuit in half and licked at the cream filling.

"Investing? I remember having a conversation with your mother many years ago. You're never too young to learn about money." As often happened, Grandad didn't lift his biscuit out of his tea in time, and a large, soggy chunk broke off, landing on the table. "Bother, I'm a messy blighter." He used his spoon to scoop it up. "So, what did your mother say?"

"Well ... you see ... I need a new skateboard ..."

"Already? You just bought one with your birthday money."

"Yeah, but that was months ago."

"You've not broken it?" Grandad gave Billy a stern look.

"No, course not. Actually, I've gotten too good." Billy beamed back at his Grandad.

"Too good? Who told you that?" Grandad's furrowed brow said he didn't feel sure about Billy being too good.

"Honest, it's a boy from the school where Mum's deputy head. He's the best skateboarder around here, and he taught me. Now, I'm nearly as good as him." Billy bit into his biscuit. "He thinks ..." Crumbs sprayed everywhere.

"Hang on, stop. Wait until you've finished chewing."

"Sorry, Granddad, it's just, I'm so excited." Billy swung his legs to and fro under the table as he talked. "He said I should enter the under-fifteens skateboard competition!"

"That's marvellous, but you're only ten."

"That's what Mum says, but it's because I'm so good."

"I don't see what that's got to do with investing." Grandad rubbed his forehead as he spoke.

"Basically, to compete, I need a better board. I've seen the one I want, but it's a hundred and forty pounds. So, Mum suggested I invest to get the money." Billy sat back in his seat.

"I still don't really understand. Invest what?"

"If you remember, I used my birthday money from you, and some of my pocket money to buy the board I have now. But I need a new, much better one."

"Okay." Grandad leant in, hoping that might help him understand. "Then what?"

"If I use this board to give other kids lessons, and if they pay me, say fifty pence or even a pound, I can save that money toward my new board."

"Ah, I see. You'll make your birthday money work for you." Grandad sat back and smiled. "I taught your mother well."

Billy bent to stroke Jacko, who lay under the table. "But, I'm not too sure how to go about it."

"Well, you have a skateboard and the ability to use it better than most of the children around here … yes?" Grandad kept a close eye on Billy; he wanted to make sure he followed each step. "So, now you need to find children who want to learn and will pay to be taught." Grandad pulled open the drawer in the kitchen table and took out a pad of paper and a pen.

Billy watched his every move.

"Right, so, who knows about these lessons?" Grandad waited to write the answer.

Billy shrugged, "No one, really. I told Ant, sort of, but no one else."

"That's what I thought." Grandad pushed the pad and pen toward Billy.

What you need to do is let everyone know, like they do on the TV—advertise."

"What, on the TV?"

"No, silly. Make a poster or two and put them where other kids will see." Grandad raised his head and looked up while he thought. "I know, put one at the skate park ramp, one in the newsagent's window, and maybe, hand out some in the school playground. You might have to ask your teacher before can you do that, though."

3

FOOTBALL AND SKATEBOARDING

"Mum, can I use the computer, please?" Billy shouted out randomly, hoping his mother, wherever she was, might hear.

A muffled, "What for?" drifted down the stairs.

Billy ran toward the sound, "I need to make some posters. Grandad told me to, for my skateboarding lessons."

After what seemed like an age, Billy's mum appeared on the landing. She had a towel wrapped around her head, turban style, and streaks of brown running down her face and onto her neck. "How many?"

Billy peered up at her but chose to say nothing about how she looked.

"Just three large ones." He didn't want to say too big a number in case she said no. "And ten small, to hand out around the playground."

"Okay, but mind the papers on my office desk. Don't just shove them to one side; it's all the marking I've got to do." She disappeared from view.

Billy set about making the skateboarding lesson posters. After he had finished printing, he left her office as he'd found it, except that he put the PTA note about tablet computers right on top of his mum's pile of papers, hoping she might see it and buy him one.

The following morning, during school assembly, Mrs Johnston, the Head Teacher, read out notices about all the activities coming up in the next few weeks.

"I have a note here from Miss Grundy, who's in charge of sports. It says the school has an opportunity to take part in the Mixed U11A football league, and at lunchtime today, she will hold trials for years five and six for any boy or girl interested in playing for the team. If you are, meet her in the sports hall at one pm."

A buzz of excitement ran around the hall, and the general noise level rose.

"Before we finish, I have one more notice." Mrs Johnston waved a highly colourful sheet of paper around. She stopped talking while she read it herself. As she did, her eyebrows moved together, and little vertical lines appeared between them. "Will Billy Field please stand up?" She looked around the hall. "Is this yours?"

Billy swallowed hard; he felt a bit light-headed. Everyone turned to look at him. "Yes, Mrs Johnston." His hesitant voice only made it a few rows in front of him. *What have I done?* He thought.

"This sounds like an enterprising scheme. Billy is offering skateboarding lessons." She showed the poster again, "So, if you want some help, you know who to ask. Oh, and Billy, good luck in the under-fifteen skateboarding championships."

Billy's face turned red all the way to the tips of his ears. His leg trembled. "Thank you, Mrs Johnston, and if anyone wants any skateboarding lessons, please find me at break-time."

"Right, boys and girls." Miss Grundy clapped her hands. The sound echoed throughout the sports hall. "Gather around, please … I see we have …" She stopped speaking while she counted, "Twenty hopefuls. I need eleven, plus two reserves for the team. As you can see, I've set up a course. I want each of you to take a ball and dribble the length of the hall, weaving in and out of the cones as you go. Once you reach the far end, pick up your ball and run back to the start, and then do the course again. I want to see ball control, speed, and stamina—that means how puffed out you feel. Form a line, and on my whistle, off you go."

The noise in the hall exploded when everyone jostled to grab a place in the queue. Tom set off first, and Billy fourth, but Ant couldn't tie his laces quickly enough and ended up at the back of the line.

Both Tom and Billy had completed one circuit before Ant had even started.

"Come on; get a move on." Tom grabbed Ant around the waist and pushed him forward. "Run, or you'll never get a place in the team."

After a few minutes of chaos, the bright orange-and-white striped cones no longer stood in neat lines but rolled haphazardly wherever they'd gotten kicked. Footballs took on a life of their own, bouncing everywhere, while children ran in all directions trying to bring theirs, or any other ball, back under their control. Miss Grundy herself came under siege by a complaining mob unable to complete the trial for one reason or another.

The high-pitched, piercing tone of a whistle, blown with all the strength she could manage, deafened those close to her while it brought everyone else to an abrupt standstill.

"I've seen enough, thank you. I'll put up a notice on the board in the main corridor.

If your name is on it, you will need to collect a permission form for away matches and a list of kit needed from the school secretary Mrs Wixen. Is that understood?"

A murmured, "Yes, Miss," followed as everyone filed out, back to their classrooms.

Billy arrived home from school with a proud smile spread across his face. He burst through the back door and into the kitchen. "Mum, Mum!" He looked around an empty room. "Where are you?" Billy dashed out into the hall.

"Here, in my study, marking homework."

Billy yanked open the door and sped through it like a high-speed train exiting a tunnel.

"Whoa, slow down." Billy's mum grabbed at her piles of books, fearing he would knock them everywhere. "What is it?"

"Me, two things." Billy spoke so fast that he didn't make any sense.

"You what?" His mum still had no idea why he'd grown so excited.

"I've got four kids for lessons, and …" He stopped to take a breath, "I got picked for the new football team to play in the Mixed U11A league!" Billy jumped up and down several times; the sheets of paper he held flapped in time with the jumps.

"Billy, that's fantastic." His mum stood, and her outstretched arms pulled him into her. She hugged him tight. "Just wait until your dad hears; he'll be so pleased."

Billy managed to wriggle free. "These are for you." He handed her the consent form and kit list.

Billy's mum quickly glanced at the form and list of kit items. "I'll take a proper look later." *More expense,* she thought, and then put them down. "Come on; let's make a special celebration tea. Dad'll get home soon."

4

SKIDDING IN THE

RAIN

Early evening, a week later, the distinctive sound of a telephone ringing filled Billy's house, accompanied by a shout from his mum.

"Can you answer that?"

Billy stood in his bedroom, modelling his new football kit. The shirt looked mostly blue with a yellow swirl running diagonally across the chest just below the neck and disappearing under the right arm to continue as a vertical line down to the waist. His school badge was stitched onto the top left front, and on the back was a large yellow number '9" for *centre-forward*. The shorts, in the same blue material, also had a vertical yellow line running up from the right leg to the waist. Billy stood in front of the wardrobe mirror and twisted himself like a corkscrew so that he could get a look at his back as well as his front.

"I'm trying on my new football kit," he called back.

The telephone continued to ring.

The strained voice of his mum came back, "Please, Billy. My rubber gloves are all wet. It's probably Dad to say he'll be late."

"Okay …" Billy ran from his room, along the landing, down the stairs, and into the kitchen. Jacko heard the commotion and stood to greet him.

"Sorry, Jacks." Billy ran past without even giving him a stroke. "I've got to get this." He lunged for the telephone just as it stopped ringing. "Bother. … Mum, I missed it." As he spoke, the answer machine came on.

This is the Royal Berkshire Hospital, A&E Department. Please ring 0118 326111. Thank you, followed by a click and silence.

"Mum!" Billy called at the top of his voice, "Quick; it's the hospital."

"I'm here. What's happened?" Billy's mum gasped as she ran down the stairs still wearing her pink rubber gloves and carrying a plastic bottle of bathroom cleaner.

"The hospital … they left a message. I couldn't get to the phone quick enough. I tried; ask Jacko."

They both listened to the answer machine. His mum dialled the number, and music sounded from the phone.

"It's busy." She held the receiver away from her ear, and the tinny sound of some old pop song blasted from it.

"Do you think it's Dad?" Billy's voice had a hint of panic, "Or Grandad? He complained about his knees the other day." Billy paled and clutched his stomach at the thought of his grandad in hospital.

"Hey, not so fast; we've no idea. ... Anyway, Grandad has to go to hospital for an operation soon, so I doubt it's him."

"What if he fell or something?" Billy looked at the telephone. "Come on; *answer.*"

"Hello, A&E Department, Nurse Collins speaking. How can I help you?" came from the telephone.

"Oh, hi, someone called from this number and left a message."

"Who's speaking, please?" The voice sounded calm and reassuring.

"Mrs Field."

"Just one moment, please."

Billy and his mum could hear the click-clack sound of a computer keyboard.

"Mrs Field, is Walter Field your husband?"

"Yes. Why, what's happened to him?" A tingle ran down her spine and Billy turned pale.

He pulled on his mum's sleeve. "What's she saying?"

"Shush. I'm trying to listen." His mum pressed the phone hard against her ear. If it was bad news, she wanted to know first without Billy overhearing.

"Mum, please tell me."

"Hold still." She turned away from Billy so that she could hear clearly. "Yes, we can come right away. It will take us about half an hour." She hung-up the phone. "Come on, Billy ... quick."

"But I've got my football kit on."

"Oh, never mind. Just grab your coat; no one will see."

"Do we need grapes?" Billy looked up at his mum as they walked from the car park and toward the hospital buildings.

"Can you see a sign? These places are always so confusing." As Billy's mum became more anxious, the lump in her throat felt more uncomfortable. "Grapes? They're for sick people." She swallowed hard.

"We don't know Dad's not. Everyone takes grapes to hospital," Billy insisted.

"Let's find out what's what first. Now, which way do we go?"

They both stood and studied the signs.

"There." Billy pointed, "The one with white writing on red. Come on, Mum." He took hold of her hand and pulled.

"Mrs Field." The nurse at reception repeated her name. "They've taken your husband to the observation ward—straight through the double doors to the end of the corridor."

Before the nurse had finished speaking, Billy's mum had grabbed his hand and set off at top speed. "Come on."

"Mum, slow down; you're hurting me."

The double doors banged behind her. "Ah, here we are." She looked around for a nurse. "Can you help me, please? I'm looking for Walter Field." Billy's mum sounded out of breath, and puffed as she spoke. "This … is … Billy."

"Nice to meet you, Billy." The ward nurse flashed him a big smile. "Now, don't fret. Your dad's had a car accident. Nothing too serious, no bones broken, but he banged his head. We just need to keep him in overnight to make sure he's okay." The nurse maintained her smile as she spoke.

Billy wondered if he should tell her she had a bit of green cabbage or something on her tooth. He couldn't stop looking at it, but he felt too worried about his dad to bother. "Can I see him? But we've no grapes."

"Yes, of course. I'm sure he won't mind about no grapes. He might seem a bit drowsy; we gave him something to help him sleep."

"There he is, Mum." Billy ran ahead. "Dad, it's us." Billy threw his arms around him.

"Steady, son; I feel a bit sore." His dad hugged him back. He tried to turn his head, but it proved too difficult. "Where's Mum?"

"You gave us a scare." Billy's mum bent and kissed her husband.

"Eww, Mum, that's gross." Billy looked away, embarrassed.

"So, what happened?" She sat close to her husband and took hold of his hand.

"Water. Well, a large puddle, really. You know that sharp corner at the bottom of Lark Hill? I came around it, not particularly fast, and the next thing I knew, the car ended up in a ditch, and some chap stood asking if I felt okay."

"Well, I'm so glad you're all right. What about your car?"

"Written off, I reckon. We'll have to wait for the insurance company."

"Cor, does that mean we get a new one?" Billy sat on the end of the bed, pretending to drive. "How about one like James Bond; they go super-fast? Go on, Dad, say yes ... please."

"I like having Dad at home." Billy sat at the kitchen table, reading his school book. He looked up at his mum and smiled.

"It's only been a day, Billy; he'll go back to work after the weekend."

"But how will he get there? He's not got a car."

"The insurance company will give us a spare one until we get a new one." His mum continued rolling out some pastry.

"Insurance? Is that like investment?" Billy wrote his name in the flour that dusted the table.

"Not really." His mum thought some more, "Well, sort of. With insurance, you pay money to a company just in case something bad happens, and if it does, they put it right. Like Dad and the car."

Billy twisted his mouth while he thought more about her answer. "What if nothing bad ever happens, and you don't get your money back? Then, you've wasted it."

"Not really; having insurance means that you've not had the worry about what would happen if the house flooded, or the car crashed, or your holiday got ruined. You take insurance out on large things that are expensive or difficult to replace like cars, houses, and holidays."

"You couldn't replace me. Have you got insurance on me?" Billy held a cheeky grin.

"Well, that's not such a silly thing to ask. Life insurance is for people, and pet insurance is for animals like Jacko."

At the mention of his name, Jacko appeared from under the table and nudged Billy's arm.

"How's my bestest dog, then?" Billy gave Jacko a big hug. "Mum has you insured." He buried his face in the dog's fur. "Haven't you?" Billy looked at his mum for reassurance.

"Yes, for some vet bills, but insurance doesn't pay for everything. With the car insurance we'll get a new one but we will still have to pay some money toward it."

5

"FETCH, JACKO"

In the garden, Billy picked up Jacko's large rubber bone and tossed it high into the air toward Ant. The dog shot off after it. Ant stood with his arms outstretched, ready to catch it. But, looking up, the sun shone directly into his face. He missed the catch.

"Butterfingers," Billy called out.

"It was the sun. I couldn't see anything." Ant rubbed his eyes.

Before the bone had finished bouncing, Jacko had it in his teeth. He settled down, resting a paw on one end, and the other end, he held tight in his mouth.

"You won't get that back from Jacks now." Billy knew his dog too well.

Ant wandered over to where the dog lay; he bent down, "Come on, boy." He put his hand out to take the bone. It looked slimy, covered in dog drool. "Let me have it."

Jacko lifted his head and stared at Ant with his big brown eyes as if to say, *if you want it, you've got to get it first*. Jacko always liked the challenge of a tug of war.

Ant, keen to avoid the drool, reached out with two fingers. Then he hooked them around the bone and pulled.

Jacko pulled against him; *surely, you can do better than that.*

Billy strolled over, "I told you that he won't give it back; he wants a game of chase. You watch." As he spoke, Billy lunged at the dog, pretending to make a grab for the bone. From a sitting position, Jacko jumped and ran to the far end of the garden. Both boys chased after him. The faster they ran, the faster Jacko ran in the opposite direction.

"We'll never catch him like this; we need a plan ... I know, you wait here, and I'll sneak around behind him. When he sees me coming, he'll run toward you. Then you grab the bone, okay." Billy walked slowly, acting casual to try and fool Jacko, but he wouldn't come anywhere near him.

Ant stood a few meters in front of Jacko, pretending to look everywhere except at the dog. Jacko settled down for a good chew.

On tiptoe, Billy managed to come right up behind the dog. He lent forward to touch his back. Jacko, with the bone, took off like a frightened rabbit. He turned his head around to see if Billy followed and ran straight into Ant. Caught off guard, Jacko gave up the bone easily.

"Quick, take it into the kitchen," Billy yelled to Ant.

Ant ran toward the back door with Billy close behind. They fell into the kitchen, trying to get away from the dog. Billy kicked at the door to slam it shut. Instead of a bang from the heavy door crashing closed, there came a loud yelp and heavy thud. Jacko's right front leg took the full force of the shutting door, and Jacko, unable to stop, barrel-rolled into it.

"No!" Billy yanked the door open wide. Jacko lay still, his leg looked mangled, and it oozed blood, matting his golden fur. Billy burst into tears, "Jacks!" He squatted beside the dog, unsure of what to do. With the dog lying on his side, Billy could see his little friend's eyes. They seemed cloudy. That meant something was badly wrong.

"Sorry, mate." Billy gulped. "I didn't mean to hurt you." He couldn't hold back his tears and let out a deafening cry. "Jacko …"

Ant dashed around the house, calling for Billy's parents. He hadn't gone far when Billy's mum appeared. She had heard all the fuss.

"Billy? What on Earth's happened?" She didn't wait for an answer. From the look of the dog crashed out by the door and the pool of blood, she knew that they needed a vet. The telephone number hung pinned to the kitchen noticeboard. She dialled quickly.

Billy felt too upset to hear; his mum listened and relayed the vet's instructions to Ant.

"Keep the dog calm and warm, and use a wet towel to lay over the injury to stop the dog licking it ..." She looked directly at Ant. "In Jacko's basket, you'll find his blanket, can you fetch it, please? Also, by the sink is a small towel. Can you wet it and bring it here. The vet's coming shortly."

"Mrs Field, Billy, we had to operate; his leg had broken, but Jacko's on the mend. Over the next few weeks, you've got to give him extra special care: no long walks, no climbing stairs, or letting him get up onto the sofa. I don't want him to jump down. Make sure he doesn't get out of the garden, and no chasing games." The vet gave Billy a stern look. "He's sleepy now from the operation, and I've got some painkillers for him." She handed a plastic jar to Billy's mum, "When he's had a dose, he will think he's better and want to play. Dogs are like two-year-old toddlers; they take no notice of what you say to them. Billy, it's down to you to make sure he behaves and gets better."

On the way back from the vet's, Billy asked his dad to stop at *Everything for Pets*. Billy's mum took her purse; Billy took a trolley.

Billy remembered what the vet had said. "We need to keep him warm and comfortable, and he'll need less food 'cos he won't be running around." Billy loaded up the trolley with a fleece dog blanket, a dog pillow, a wicker basket with a low side so that Jacko didn't have to step so high, a new smaller feeding bowl, some non-slip dog socks for indoors, and for going in the garden, water resistant dog boots.

"I think that's enough now, Billy. Jacko's accident is working out quite expensive."

"But, Mum, we want him to get better. Poor Jacks."

"Of course we do. He might be a pet, but he's part of the family."

"And we love him … loads," Billy added.

"Yes, we do, very much, but with your new football kit and your tablet computer …"

"Tablet computer! Am I getting one?" Billy rushed over and threw his arms around his mum. "Thanks, Mum." He hugged her tight.

"As I was saying, plus having to pay toward Dad's new car, and now Jacko's vet bills, it's all getting too expensive." Her voice sounded heavy with worry.

Across the car park, Billy could see his dad sat in the rear of the new estate car, keeping Jacko company while he waited for them to return.

Jacko heard their voices and tried to lift his head. It proved too much for him, and all he could manage was a swish of his large brush tail.

"See, he's getting better." Billy so wanted to hug his dog but knew he mustn't excite him. He settled for giving him a scratch behind the ear. If Jacko could, he would have smiled.

6

BIONIC GRANDAD

Billy, Ant, and Tom shared the same table in Miss Tompkins' year five class.

"Today, we are looking at robots as part of our design and technology work." Miss Tompkins peered over the top of her glasses at her class. "Can anyone tell me about robots? Now, don't just shout out, put up your hand first."

A forest of arms reached for the sky, but Billy thrust his arm so hard upwards that his bottom lifted clear off his seat. "Miss, Miss ... ask me, Miss. Pleeeeaaase."

"Well, Billy, it looks like I'd better ask you before you burst."

"I'm not sure if it's quite the same thing, Miss, but my grandad is going to be bionic!" Billy looked at Ant and Tom for their reactions. They both sniggered.

"What's he on about?" Tom said from behind his hand so that Miss wouldn't hear. Ant shrugged.

Miss Tompkins' eyes bulged, and her eyebrows disappeared into her hairline. "Bionic, you say? What do you mean, your grandad will be bionic?"

"It's true, Miss. He's got to have both knees replaced with new titanium ones, I think it's called. It'll mean he'll be able to run at over a hundred miles an hour."

All the children in the class laughed.

"I think your grandad may be playing a joke on you." Miss smiled.

"Well, me and Mum have to take him to the hospital next week, then he'll come and live with us while he gets better."

"I'm sure he is going in for a knee operation, but I'm not sure he'll be able to run at a hundred miles per hour afterward."

"Maybe, Miss." Billy looked down at his desk. "I bet he will," he said under his breath. "'Cos he's a special grandad."

The downstairs hallway in Billy's house was stacked high with tables, chairs, books, vases, china figures, and all sorts from where Billy and his dad had removed the furniture from the dining room.

Through the front door, Billy's dad staggered, carrying Grandad's favourite comfy armchair. "It turned out to be a bit of luck that I crashed the car and got the estate; otherwise, we'd have had to hire a van to move this lot." He plonked the chair in a space near the bottom of the stairs and smiled at Billy.

"Dad, don't say that. What would have happened if it had been really bad and you had died or something?"

"I know, sorry, Billy. I shouldn't joke like that. I'll need your help to get the mattress in from the car." His dad squeezed Billy's arm muscles. "Mum told me how strong you are, carrying those potatoes."

"Will Grandad stay long?"

"That's a strange question." His dad frowned; deep lines formed between his eyes. "You love your grandad … he's the only one you've got."

"Yes, of course, but if he's to live in our dining room, we won't be able to use it. That's what I meant." Billy collected up several more ornaments and placed them with the rest. "It's just that the dining room always reminds me of your mum, granny Nana Field. Whenever she came around, she always bought yummy cakes, and she told us loads of stories about her being a little girl. She was my favourite granny, and I miss her." Billy let a small tear roll down his cheek.

"I miss her too, son." His dad put his arm around Billy's shoulders and gave him a squeeze. "That's why we need to look after Grandad. Once he has new knees, he won't be able to do much for himself for six weeks or more. You'll have to act as his legs."

"And Jacko," Billy offered. "If we make a tray with ropes and tie it to Jacko's back, then we can get him to carry stuff from the kitchen to Grandad's bedside."

"Not at the moment. Poor chap still has a limp. Have you seen Jacko trying to stand up? He can't put any weight on his leg."

"I didn't mean to hurt him, Dad; we were just playing." Billy felt sick inside at the reminder of Jacko's broken leg. He thought some more, "I know, if we put Jacko in bed with Grandad, they can get better together." Billy laughed at his idea.

Soon after his operation, Grandad came back to live in Billy's house while he got better. Each day, a lady came to make sure he exercised his legs, and afterward, Grandad felt exhausted. He liked to sit in his favourite chair next to his bed. Jacko never strayed far away. Billy would race home from school to join them both.

"Here you are, Grandad." Billy came into the dining room with a mug of tea." I've brought you one digestive biscuit so that you don't get even fatter." Billy's smirk told Grandad that he'd meant it as a joke.

"You are a shocker, young Billy." Grandad pretended to feel annoyed. "Don't you know that digestive biscuits have magic healing powers, and are recommended for people with new knees?" He tried hard not to smile.

"Is that like you being able to run a hundred miles an hour with your bionic legs?" Billy knew that his Grandad kidded with him and sat on the bed while he drank his tea and ate his custard cream. Jacko sat on the floor, staring up at both, hoping a crumb might fall his way.

"Grandad, can I ask you something?"

"Anything."

"Mum told me that she would get me a tablet computer for school. That was weeks ago, and she hasn't yet. Do you think she's forgotten?" Billy bit into his biscuit.

"You need to ask her, but I know your mum and dad have had lots of bills recently, and those gadgets are so expensive."

"About five hundred pounds, but she did promise." Billy took a lick of the cream filling.

"And I'm sure she meant it, but maybe she's got to save up some money. That's the problem with money; it's too easy to spend but much more difficult to get in the first place. That's why people go to work."

Billy and Grandad sat in silence while Jacko snuffled, snorted, and yawned occasionally, like dogs do.

"By the way, Billy, how's your investment going? Did you get any children to pay for skateboarding lessons?"

"I've got …" Billy pulled a sheet of paper from his schoolbag, "One, two, three ..." He counted some more. "Ten who want lessons."

"Ten? That sounds good."

"Yeah, but I've only got four pounds toward my new skateboard, not including my pocket money." He looked disappointed.

"How come?"

"'Cos some say can I bring the money next week, or something like that, and then they don't." Billy's usual smile changed to a sullen expression. "What can I do, Grandad?"

"You'll have to become more firm. Say, "no money, no lesson". Like all small businesses …"

"Me, a small business." Billy sat up straight and pushed his chest out. A smile returned to his face. "Am I a business person?" He said it out loud.

"You are, young Billy; how exciting is that? What shall we call your business?"

"Billy's Business, no … um, how about Billy Field's Best Ever Business."

"I'm not sure about that. Let's stick to Billy Field Enterprises. Now, we've got to think of new ways to get more money."

7

CATS IN DEVON

During school assembly, Tom looked about before bending down to open his school bag. Ant and Billy were sat either side listening to Mrs Johnston talking about the new lunchtime rota.

Tom gestured to Billy and Ant to take a look into his bag. "It's a new games controller," he mouthed. Both boys leant forward for a better look.

"Is it yours?" Billy whispered.

'… The juniors will have preference, and to make sure the queues are kept in order, I need senior children to supervise them." Mrs Johnston raised her voice. "Who will volunteer?"

"Look out!" Billy flashed his eyes left. He saw Miss Tompkins walking toward the back of the hall where they sat. "Wait 'til break-time."

Back home that evening, standing at the kitchen sink, Billy had a mound of potatoes and bunch of carrots to prepare. He scrubbed off the mud and set about removing the carrot tops.

"Mum, I've noticed how much difference one extra person makes since Grandad's been living here. It takes ages to sort the veg now." Billy counted out the potatoes. "I think I've done enough."

"I don't know what I'd do without my star chef." Billy's mum came over to look at what he'd prepared. "Yes, that'll do. You're a real help, Billy."

"Mum …"

"Yes?"

"At school today, you know Tom, well, he had an awesome games controller."

"Did he? That's nice." His mum continued to chop an onion.

"It's much better than my old one. You should've seen it." Billy got more excited as he spoke.

"Oh, well, maybe you should put it on your birthday or Christmas list."

"But, Mum, they're aaaaages away. It's the latest; everyone at school's getting one."

"And who, exactly, is everyone?" She looked directly at him.

"Tom ... "

"And?"

"Ant wants one. So do Khalid and Julie. They all said so at break-time."

"So, Tom's got one, you say. Was it for his birthday, or did he buy it with his own money?"

"Well, actually, it's his brother Eddy's. Tom just brought it in to school to show us." Billy stopped to think. "You know you said I'm your star chef; maybe you could buy it for me now. I'd be really cool at school if you did." Billy cocked his head to one side and stared toward his mum. She had tears streaming down her cheeks. "Mum, what's up?" He ran over and put his arm around her. "Don't get upset." Billy remembered what his grandad had said to him about his mum and dad having to pay out a lot of money. He didn't want her to get worried or sad. "I don't need a new controller; it's just Tom's looked mega."

His mum took a scrap of tissue from her pocket. "It's not the money." She blew her nose. "It's 'cos I'm chopping onions. They always make me cry." She dabbed her cheek. Billy didn't feel so sure it was the onions.

"Does that mean you'll buy me a new controller?" Billy pulled another tissue from the box on the side and gave it to her.

"No, sorry, Billy. We need to be careful with money now with all the extra expenses." She blew her nose one more time. "We've been meaning to tell you something."

"What?" Billy screwed up his face; he didn't like the sound of that.

"You remember at Christmas, when we talked about going to Disneyland this summer ..."

"I know, I'm so excited, I've told everyone." Billy pretended to bounce a ball and threw it into a basketball hoop like American kids he'd seen on TV.

"Well, we can't afford it. I've had to cancel the holiday. Sorry."

"Oh, Mum! I've told everyone we're going to America." Billy stamped his foot. "It's not fair."

"Sometimes, life seems unfair, Billy, but we had to fix Jacko's leg and help Dad with the car. Those things were more important. But, hey, it's not so bad. We're still going on holiday. Dad and I have arranged to go to Devon."

"Devon! That's poo." Billy curled his top lip. "That's no fun at all."

"Well, because we've got the new estate car, we can take Jacko. He couldn't have come to America." She looked at Billy. "Jacko gets a holiday now too. That's good, isn't it? I think he deserves it after what happened to him."

"Suppose so." Billy ground his back teeth.

"And Grandad can come." His mum sounded even more cheery.

Billy forced a smile. "Are we going to a holiday camp or a mega-posh hotel?" The thought of either made him feel much happier.

"Well, not exactly." His mum hesitated. "You know your Auntie May …"

"Oh, Mum, not Auntie May and Auntie June's." Billy threw a potato into the sink.

"Billy! Now, less of that. You like your aunties, and they always send you Christmas and birthday presents."

"I know. It's not them but their hundreds of cats." Billy slunk across the kitchen, toward the hall, and up the stairs to his bedroom.

"Fourteen at last count, actually."

"Yeah, but they stink, and make loads of mess."

"Billy, can you come back here, please?" His mum stood in the middle of the kitchen. He came and stood in front of her.

"Now, look at me." She put her finger under his chin and lifted his head. "I need you to understand that you can't always have what you want. At times, we all have to make compromises like getting that own-brand shower gel instead of the Spiderman one, or going to Devon and not Disneyland. There are loads of things I'd like to buy and places to go, but for different reasons, I can't. You've seen adverts on the telly for exotic faraway islands, or expensive cars with soft leather heated seats and TV's built into the headrests ..."

"Cor, can we have a car like that?" Billy's eyes sparkled at the idea.

"No, you're not hearing me. I work at Elliott's school, and Dad works in the council offices. We both get paid money each month. It's called a salary. Do you understand?" She brought her face close to his.

"Yeah, but why can't we have a car with TV's in the back?"

"That's what I'm trying to tell you. From our salaries, we have to buy everything—food, heating, lights, TV, Internet, mortgage ..."

"What's a mortgage, Mum?" Billy wore a puzzled expression.

"To live in a house or flat, you need to pay for it, like everyone else. You can either rent it or buy it. We chose to buy this house, but houses cost thousands of pounds."

"How many thousands? Two, three, more?" Billy asked, optimistically.

"Try two hundred and fifty thousand pounds," she spoke slowly. "That's the number 25, followed by four noughts."

Billy's mouth fell open. "Mum, that's crazy. That's like from here to the moon!"

"When we got married, we didn't have that much money, so we borrowed it from the bank. Of course, they want it back, which means each month, for the next twenty-five years, we'll pay a regular sum. That's a mortgage."

"Twenty-five years. I'll be well grown up by then." He counted on his fingers. "I'll be thirty-five years old. That's ancient."

"And married with children, and a mortgage of your own, most likely." His mum smiled.

"I'm never going to get a mortgage. I'll live in a tent or build a camp down the woods."

"We'll see. Wait until you're older, and you've got a good job …"

"Or Billy Field Enterprises becomes a success." Billy stood up tall, thinking about his business.

His mum took a step back. "What's that, then?"

"Grandad asked me about my skateboarding lessons, and I told him that kids want them, but they're not bringing their money. He said that happens a lot to small businesses. He reckons that's what I am—a small business—so we named it Billy Field Enterprises."

TWENTY-POUND

NOTE

The Saturday of the skateboarding competition arrived. In the park, surrounding the half-pipe ramp, crowds of people gathered. Ant, with his sister Max, Tom with his sister Katie, Max's best friend, Khalid, Julie, and an assortment of Billy's classmates. They'd all gone there to watch the events and cheer Billy on—the youngest ever contender in the under-fifteens competition. Even his teacher, Miss Tompkins, had turned up.

The owner of the *Boards and Bikes* shop, who'd organised the event, sorted out the groups of riders. As well as the competitions, he had arranged for a van selling hot food and drinks, and an ice-cream van to come, plus he had set up a temporary shop selling loads of skateboarding stuff, and organised a St Johns Ambulance First Aid tent in case of accidents.

The younger and less skilful children would go first, and since Billy was in the under-fifteens, the highlight of the competition, he had to wait until much later in the day before competing. The older boys stood near the ramp, chatting while they waited.

"Well done, mate." Dan, a year nine boy from Elliott's school, slapped Billy on the back. "It was only a few months ago that we met and you had never ridden a proper board before." Dan turned to his brother Woody. "Would you believe it? And now you're here competing against me, and on my old board." Dan took up the board he'd sold Billy. "This was my favourite, but I don't think it's fast enough to win the competition."

"We'll see. I had hoped to get an Element Nyjah Weaver, but they cost a hundred and forty pounds," Billy said.

"Yeah, a great board; we all want one of them." Dan and Woody nodded in agreement at Billy's choice. "I thought you were giving lessons to get the money. Smart idea; I've seen the posters."

Billy pulled himself up tall. "Yeah, I've been doing some, but I've not saved enough money yet."

Tom had stood listening.

"Billy would have, but he spent fifty quid on a new games controller like my brother's."

Billy looked first at Dan and back to Tom. He then dropped his head and stared at his board, hoping somehow it might turn in an Element Nyjah Weaver.

"You can't have everything, Billy," Dan remarked.

"You sound like my mum." Billy laughed.

"She's our deputy head. I like your mum. Maybe you should listen to her." Dan gave Billy another playful slap on the back. "Have you seen the time?" Dan held up his watch, "We're on soon. Come on."

The lads set off, as cheers of *good luck Billy, fingers crossed,* and, *you can do it* came from Tom, Ant, and his school friends.

The five competitors in the under-fifteen group stood on the platform above the half-pipe, looking at what lay before them, including the crowds surrounding the skate park. Seeing everyone watching caused Billy's stomach to whirl like a washing machine, his legs to shake, and everything he knew about skateboarding to leave his brain in an instant. As the youngest, the organisers decided he would go last. It didn't help him, as now he would have to watch the older boys drop, pump, kick, twist, and perform all the other clever things they could do.

Billy thought about the four contenders; Stu and Dan, and how good they were, but the other two lads were strangers. He remembered seeing the one holding an Element Nyjah Weaver board and dreaming of owning one when in the supermarket car park with his mum. *Competing against this lot,* Billy thought, *I haven't much of a chance.*

As a previous three-times winner, Stu went first. Billy had only seen Stu when he taught, but now his skills and speed shone through. His style and choice of tricks had everyone spell-bound. He was the master. And watching him did nothing for Billy's confidence. *You can do it*, Billy told himself; *remember how you played the Keymaster in the school play.*

When Stu finished, the clapping, whistles, shouts, and cat-calls left no doubt in Billy's mind who was champion.

Dan went next. He seemed different from Stu, more relaxed, just easing his board around the curves before going into an Ollie jump, and then dropping perfectly for his next race across the half-pipe to complete even more tricks. He received enthusiastic clapping from his brother, and from a group of girls standing off to one side.

The two unknown boys did all right but nothing outstanding compared to Stu and

Dan; however, compared to himself, Billy still needed to do a lot of practicing. His smile vanished.

Stu noticed Billy's glum expression. "Remember, Billy, you're only ten, and you've made it into this competition—you're a winner already." Stu's words gave him the encouragement he needed to do his best.

Billy's first drop off the platform edge had a lot of importance. Nervous, standing and leaning backward slightly with all his weight on his back foot and the board's tail, Billy waited for the signal to go. It came; he pushed forward; the air rushed against his face. His instincts took over, and the inner voice of doubt became lost in the roar of the crowd. He dropped into the half-pipe with great speed and stability. His balance perfect, he completed a grind followed by a tail-slide faultlessly. Then he gathered speed for an Ollie jump and raced across the half-pipe. Before he knew it, all four wheels rose in the air, and his left hand had a firm grip on the board. The landing felt smooth, and his confidence rose. He wanted to end on a kick-flip; nothing too spectacular but impressive to watch. It didn't go as he'd hoped it would, and he and his board went separate ways. Everyone felt the thud of Billy hitting the floor of the half-pipe.

"Cor, I bet that hurt," Ant said to Tom. Both boys winced and rubbed their own bums as if they had fallen.

Unconcerned, Billy jumped to his feet. He retrieved his board, and held it high in the air while taking a bow. Caught up in the excitement, Miss Tompkins let out a whoop, and all Billy's classmates followed her lead.

The noise ended when the owner of *Boards and Bikes* made an announcement over the speaker system.

"We've had a great day here," he said. "And we've seen some excellent demonstrations of skateboarding skills, and I think you'll all agree, a future skateboarding star." He pointed in the direction of Billy. The clapping and calling started again. "I need to announce the winner of the under-fifteens. It was a close-run thing between Stu Dunderdale and Dan Prescott. Stu just beat Dan, and so, for the fourth year running, I declare Stu the winner."

Stu collected his winner's trophy and held it up for everyone to see. Everyone but Tom and Ant whistled and clapped. They had wanted Billy to win.

"Before we finish," the owner of Boards and Bikes said. "I have a special award for Billy Field." Once again, the cheers filled the air. "Billy, I've decided to award you a prize for the best newcomer, and for being the youngest competitor in the under-fifteens ever." He held an envelope above his head and waved it in Billy's direction: he was watching from the opposite platform of the half-pipe. Billy dropped and pumped his way to the where the owner of Boards and Bikes stood. He did a perfect Ollie, and with his spare hand, grabbed the envelope to cries of, *go for it Billy, you're the best,* and, *awesome.*

"You should have seen me." Billy sat in front of his grandad. "I really missed you not being there."

"I wanted to come, but I can only manage about a hundred-meter walk, and then I need to rest for a good while." Grandad's mouth turned down, and he let out a heavy sigh. "Anyway, did you win?"

"Not really … " Billy put on a miserable face also. Grandad noticed.

"I am sorry. Never mind, there is always a next time."

"But I did get a special prize for best newcomer!" Billy jumped up and down several times, waving the envelope around. He beamed from ear-to-ear.

"You're a shocker, Billy Field. Always joking me." Grandad grasped Billy and pulled him to himself. "What did you get? Go on, open it." Grandad grew as excited as Billy.

"It's probably just a voucher for *Boards and Bikes*. They ran the competition." Billy held the envelope toward the light, trying to see what it held. He hadn't wanted to open it until he'd shown his grandad.

"Come on; get on with it, or we'll never know."

Billy slid his finger along the envelope's seal and peered in. His mouth formed an "O", his eyes opened wide, and his eyebrows shot up his forehead. "Grandad, you'll never guess in a million years!" Billy ran off toward the kitchen, looking for his mum. Jacko joined in the chase, limping along behind.

His mum sat studying a recipe book. She looked up, "So, what's all the excitement?"

"Here's my prize." Billy pulled out the contents of the envelope and waved it in front of her.

He had a twenty-pound note. "Billy!" His mum clasped his face in her hands. "Hold on to it this time; not like your birthday twenty-pound note."

Grandad had made it to the kitchen. "Well, I never. What a lucky boy. Another twenty-pound note."

"It's not luck, Grandad, it's skill. I've practiced for months, and I had a good teacher in Stu. If only I hadn't spent fifty pounds on that games controller, then I could have had my Element Nyjah Weaver skateboard for the competition, and I might have won."

"There's a lesson there, Billy." His grandad took hold of both shoulders and looked into his eyes, "You might want it all, but now you realise you cannot have everything without working and saving. And you have to choose what's most important to you, and what you want to buy first."

Billy thought hard about what had happened over the past few days and decided he would look after his money better.

"The twenty-pound prize will go toward the cost of the skateboard, as well as the money I earn from giving skateboarding lessons."

Grandad nodded his approval.

"I know I want a skateboard, but I need to do other things with my money."

Grandad moved his head to one side, and furrows appeared on his brow.

"Mum and Dad have spent loads recently, so I'm going to give Mum the money back for the dog bone. That way, I'll be investing in Jacko's health." *And giving something to someone else in need, which makes me feel all nice inside*, he thought.

"I'm sure they'll appreciate that." Grandad held an ear-to-ear smile.

"I'll keep a little bit of my pocket money for myself to spend now; perhaps on some sweets or something for school," Billy said.

"But I've learnt that being careful with money makes a lot of sense."

"And now you can understand how much your mum and dad do for you." Grandad looked to Billy's mum. She smiled and nodded back.

Jacko pushed in between Billy and Grandad. "And, I think someone else has gotten a lot better." Billy bent and ruffled the dog's fur. "You're my bestest dog ever, and I can't wait to go on holiday with you."

THE END

WHAT YOU CAN LEARN FROM 'BILLY WANTS IT ALL."

Money is essential because it is the means by which we obtain those things we both need and want, and without money, our society would not function.

It is important that children learn both the *purpose* and *value* of money, and how it fits into the way they live when they become adults. Parents take care of their children's financial needs until they leave education, but from then on, a child needs to become independent financially. It is sometimes a painful lesson because, while they don't have to worry about money, they can get easily misled into a false sense of security. That is, food always appears on the table when they feel hungry, and clothes in their cupboard or gifts on birthdays and at Christmas. However, the most important lesson a child has to learn is that these things don't appear from nowhere. Someone has to exchange their services—work at a job—to earn the money to purchase the goods.

Once a child gets old enough to understand the concept of money, they can begin to learn about managing it by getting given pocket money to control and spend. This can teach them that they can buy something they want right now, but that saving is an important part of the money management process. They should learn to save toward something they really want to purchase, and to invest—turning an initial sum into a larger amount over time—for the future. It is also useful to ask them to put a small percentage to one side to give to a charitable cause so that they learn from an early age to share their good fortune with people less fortunate than themselves.

As children get older, their needs and wants get larger. As they get old enough to earn money for themselves, parents can keep them focussed on the value of money by offering to pay a percentage toward an item, and have them save or earn a significant amount themselves. This works from a small item that costs less than a pound to larger items, such as bicycles or even cars. If your eighteen-year-old wants a car and knows that they have to work to get a percentage, even if still at school and with limited time, they will do whatever it takes to reach their goal. And offering to pay 75% of the car if they earn 25% will prove a much more positive experience than purchasing the car 100% for the child.

In the story, Billy wants a skateboard. He doesn't understand why he just can't have it bought for him. He doesn't have to pay anything toward any other costs in the household, so why does he have to participate in the cost of a toy? This provides the ideal time for a lesson in money management. However, it's not an easy lesson to learn and a slightly painful one for a child. Once Billy understood the value of money and how important it is to participate in acquiring it, he learned a lesson that will stand him in good stead for the rest of his life.

He understood the challenges his parents faced, and it made him respect them more and understand how much they work to invest in their family. He could even share in the family budget by offering to pay for Jacko's bone himself. It's never too early to understand and learn how to manage finances.

Never spend your money before you have earned it. **Thomas Jefferson**

A penny saved is a penny earned. **Benjamin Franklin**

GET YOUR FREE ACTIVITY BOOK

To accompany all the Billy Books there is a free activity book for each title. Each book includes word search, crossword, secret message, mazes and cryptogram puzzles plus pictures to colour.

To get your **free** Activity Book go to **www.thebillybooks.co.uk** and click the button **Get Your Free Activity Book**. Then click the cover of the book matching this book

BOOK REVIEW

If you found this book helpful, leaving a review on Goodreads.com or other book related websites would be much appreciated by me and others who have yet to find it.

READ ON FOR A TASTER OF

BILLY KNOWS A SECRET

BILLY GROWING UP SERIES; SECRETS

James Minter

Helen Rushworth – Illustrator

www.thebillybooks.com

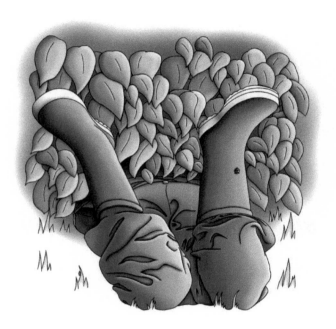

1

MAX'S BIRTHDAY
SURPRISE

On Saturday, Billy went to his best friend's house to play. He and Ant worked in the garden, building a maze for Cinders, Ant and Max's rabbit. At school, Billy and Ant had been learning about how you can teach a mouse to run through a maze and thought it would be fun to see if they could train the rabbit in the same way. The idea was to see if Cinders would find her way to the end of the maze using food as bait.

Billy and Ant had the task of making a challenging maze using anything they could find. Max, Ant's sister, had the job of chopping up a carrot to lay it as a trail in the labyrinth of corridors, including a large enticing carrot chunk placed at the far end of the maze. Once the rabbit was set free, Max also needed to make sure Cinders didn't run away, and if she did, to fetch her back.

All three children soon realised that rabbits aren't good when it comes to learning. Instead of following the path, Cinders just hopped on top of the nearest brick, paint tin, or log to sniff the air before taking a shortcut to the carrot reward.

Holding her prize between her teeth Cinders would run off to find a hiding place at the far side of the garden to eat it in safety.

After several goes, Billy and Ant went looking for extra-high obstacles to stop Cinders from running away while Max set off, yet again, to retrieve her.

Moving quietly around the garden, looking under all the bushes, Max spotted Cinders hidden amongst the thick cover of the garden hedge. The only way for her to reach the rabbit was to lay on her stomach like a soldier and drag herself along, using her elbows and knees. She did, until all that showed were the ends of her legs and feet. For anyone standing nearby, it looked like the hedge had eaten her.

As the boys wandered about in search of more maze building materials, Billy noticed a movement out of the corner of his eye. It was Ant's mum stood at the back door, waving her arms and generally behaving oddly.

"What's wrong with your mum?" Billy asked Ant. "See." He pointed at her, and both boys stared. She appeared to be looking for someone or something. Ant's mum was bent forward with her head pushed out like a tortoise. Moving from side-to-side, every now and then, she made a 'come hither' gesture.

Once she saw the boys staring, she waved frantically with one hand while putting a finger to her pursed lips with the other.

"Do you want me, Mum?" Ant called out.

"Shush," she hissed back. "Yes, both of you," she mouthed, as she scanned up and down the garden one more time.

Unsure of why they did it, but it seemed like the right thing to do, Ant and Billy looked about them before crouching and scurrying over to where Ant's mum stood.

"What is it?" Ant whispered.

"Where's Max?" his mum whispered back. "I don't want her to know." As she spoke, Ant's mum retreated into the kitchen, pulling the boys with her. She closed the back door behind them.

"What are you doing, Mum?" Ant looked first to her, and then to Billy. He shrugged.

"It's Max; she mustn't find out." Her voice came out as little more than a whisper.

"Find out what?"

"Her birthday …"

Ant pulled back and screwed up his face. "Too late; she'll be nine in a couple of weeks, and she knows all about birthdays, Mum."

"No, Ant, of course she knows it's her birthday soon, but what she doesn't know is what present she's getting."

To make sure that Max wasn't coming, her mum stood on tip-toe and took another look down the garden.

Ant reassured her. "Don't worry about her, Mum, Cinders is right under the hedge and won't come out until she's finished eating her carrot,"

"Good, because I need your help." She looked directly at Ant. "And yours, Billy."

"Our help?" the boys said together.

"Do you remember a few months back when Max painted her bike?"

"Mum, how could we forget. And the shed, and her head, and most of the bathroom." Ant laughed.

"Well, she ruined her bike, so Dad and I thought we'd get her a new one for her birthday."

"Cor, does that mean if I paint my old games controller, you'll buy me a new one?" Ant beamed up at his mum.

"If you paint your controller, you'll have no controller, no pocket money, and be grounded for a month." His mum returned a stern glare. "We're not rewarding bad behaviour; Max is getting a new bike because she's grown out of her old one. You look, the seat's already adjusted as high as it will go."

Ant's mum checked out the window again to see where Max had gotten to. She leant in and lowered her voice; the boys copied her. "I think we've all learned that she doesn't want a girlie bike, but what we don't know is what she wants her new bike to look like. That's for you two to find out, but without letting on. Her birthday bike must be a surprise. This is our secret, so you've got to promise me you won't tell her." Ant's mum creased her eyes and looked into each boy's face in turn, "Promise."

The boys nodded repeatedly.

"I want to hear you say it ..."

"I promise, Mum," came from Ant

"And you, Billy."

"I promise, Mrs Turner." Billy's tummy fluttered, and his cheeks turned pink; he wasn't sure why.

"If she finds out ..." Ant's mum wagged her finger and looked serious. "There'll be consequences."

"Ant ... Billy," Max shouted at the top of her voice while she ran up the garden, clasping Cinders. "Where are you?"

"Quick, boys!" Ant's mum opened the back door and, rather forcefully, helped them out. "Now, remember your promise," she warned.

"We're here." Ant ran toward his sister. "Who's a naughty rabbit?" He reached out to stroke Cinders laying in Max's arms.

"No, she's not. That's a stupid game. I won't let you do your maze thing anymore." Max opened the rabbit hutch door and lifted Cinders in. "And you'd better clear all that stuff away." She pointed to the collection of bricks, tins, wood, and other items. "Or else Dad'll get angry."

"Okay, bossy-boots." Ant wandered over to the maze. "Come on, Billy; you heard what she said." Ant looked around to see if Max was nearby. He put his hand to his mouth just to make sure she couldn't hear. "How will we find out which bike she wants without letting on?"

"What about taking her to the shopping centre, you know, *Boards and Bikes*? I'll pretend I'm looking for a new skateboard, and you can take Max to look at bikes. What do you reckon?" Billy smiled at his idea.

"*Boards and Bikes*? No way. Max won't go anywhere near there after having to apologise for stealing those stickers. She thinks the owner will be nasty to her." Ant's brow furrowed as he thought some more. "I know, what about getting a copy of their catalogue instead. Haven't you got one?"

"Actually, their latest one came yesterday." Billy dropped the two bricks he held and headed toward his bike. "I'll zoom home and get it now, and we can pretend to go through it. Max is always miss-nosey-pants, and she'll want to join in. I'll be real quick," he called back over his shoulder.

Both boys sat on Ant's bedroom floor, huddled around the *Boards and Bikes* catalogue. They flicked through the pages, and every once in a while, they'd make exaggerated *whoops* or *ahs* or *look at that, it's awesome* type noises. They spoke loudly, with the bedroom door open, knowing it wouldn't take long for Max to come to stick her nose in.

Sure enough she arrived. "Let me see." Max squatted beside them and grabbed for the catalogue.

"Get off, Max; this is boys' stuff. Anyway, you don't like skateboarding." Ant snatched it back.

"I might do. I saw girls doing it when we watched Billy in that competition." She pulled the magazine back toward her and turned over a page. "See there." She pointed, "I haven't got a skateboard, but I've got a bike." She bent forward for a closer look.

"I know," Billy said. "Let's pretend we've got a million pounds and can buy anything we like." His eyes sparkled at the idea. "What would you buy, Max?" Billy gave Ant a sneaky tap on his shoulder behind Max's back. Ant gave him a secret thumbs-up.

Max picked up a pencil from the floor. "I'll put an 'M' next to all the things I want." She studied each page and wrote several Ms.

"It's your go, Ant." She pushed the catalogue toward him. "You write an 'A' next to stuff you want."

Ant worked his way through the magazine page by page and noticed that Max had put Ms against two different bikes. "Sis, you can't have two bikes."

"Yes, I can. With a million pounds, I can have as many bikes as I like."

"I suppose so, but which is your favourite?" Ant gave her back the catalogue.

She drew a big circle around a Raleigh Mountain Bike.

"That's my bestest one," Max said.

"Nice," Both boys agreed, nodding their approval.

"It's my go now," Billy said. He picked up the catalogue and checked his watch. "Actually, I told Mum I wouldn't be late. I'd better get going."

Ant gave Billy a quizzical look.

"I'll show your Mum on my way out," Billy mouthed to Ant.

He reacted with a wink. "See ya, mate."

Max saw nothing.

I HOPE YOU ENJOYED THIS FREE CHAPTER. PLEASE READ 'BILLY KNOWS A SECRET." TO FIND OUT WHAT HAPPENS NEXT...

FOR PARENTS, TEACHERS, AND GUARDIANS: ABOUT THE "BILLY GROWING UP" SERIES

Billy and his friends are children entering young adulthood, trying to make sense of the world around them. Like all children, they are confronted by a complex, diverse, fast-changing, exciting world full of opportunities, contradictions, and dangers through which they must navigate on their way to becoming responsible adults.

What underlies their journey are the values they gain through their experiences. In early childhood, children acquire their values by watching the behaviour of their parents. From around eight years old onwards, children are driven by exploration, and seeking independence; they are more outward looking. It is at this age they begin to think for themselves, and are capable of putting their own meaning to feelings, and the events and experiences they live through. They are developing their own identity.

The Billy Growing Up series supports an initiative championing Values-based Education, (VbE) founded by Dr Neil Hawkes*. The VbE objective is to influence a child's capacity to succeed in life by encouraging them to adopt positive values that will serve them during their early lives, and sustain them throughout their adulthood. Building on the VbE objective, each Billy book uses the power of traditional storytelling to contrast negative behaviours with positive outcomes to illustrate, guide, and shape a child's understanding of the importance of values.

This series of books help parents, guardians and teachers to deal with the issues that challenge children who are coming of age. Dealt with in a gentle way through storytelling, children begin to understand the challenges they face, and the importance of introducing positive values into their everyday lives. Setting the issues in a meaningful context helps a child to see things from a different perspective. These books act as icebreakers, allowing easier communication between parents, or other significant adults, and children when it comes to discussing difficult subjects. They are suitable for KS2, PSHE classes.

There are eight books are in the series. Suggestions for other topics to be dealt with in this way are always welcome. To this end, contact the author by email: james@jamesminter.com.

*Values-Based Education, (VbE) is a programme that is being adopted in schools to inspire adults and pupils to embrace and live positive human values. In English schools, there is now a Government requirement to teach British values. More information can be found at: www.valuesbasededucation.com/

BILLY GETS BULLIED

Bullies appear confident and strong. That is why they are scary and intimidating. Billy loses his birthday present, a twenty-pound note, to the school bully. With the help of a grown-up, he manages to get it back and the bully gets what he deserves.

BILLY AND ANT FALL OUT

False pride can make you feel so important that you would rather do something wrong than admit you have made a mistake. In this story, Billy says something nasty to Ant and they row. Ant goes away and makes a new friend, leaving Billy feeling angry and abandoned. His pride will not let him apologise to his best friend until things get out of hand.

BILLY IS NASTY TO ANT

Jealousy only really hurts the person who feels it. It is useful to help children accept other people's successes without them feeling vulnerable. When Ant wins a school prize, Billy can't stop himself saying horrible things. Rather than being pleased for Ant, he is envious and wishes he had won instead.

BILLY AND ANT LIE

Lying is very common. It's wrong, but it's common. Lies are told for a number of different reasons, but one of the most frequent is to avoid trouble. While cycling to school, Billy and Ant mess around and lie about getting a flat tyre to cover up their lateness. The arrival of the police at school regarding a serious crime committed earlier that day means their lie puts them in a very difficult position.

BILLY HELPS MAX

Stealing is taking something without permission or payment. Children may steal for a dare, or because they want something and have no money, or as a way of getting attention. Stealing shows a lack of self-control. Max sees some go-faster stripes for her bike. She has to have them, but her birthday is ages away. She eventually gives in to temptation.

BILLY SAVES THE DAY

Children need belief in themselves and their abilities, but having an inflated ego can be detrimental. Lack of self-belief holds them back, but overpraising leads to unrealistic expectations. Billy fails to audition for the lead role in the school play, as he is convinced he is not good enough.

BILLY WANTS IT ALL

The value of money is one of the most important subjects for children to learn and carry with them into adulthood, yet it is one of the least-taught subjects. Billy and Ant want skateboards, but soon realise a reasonable one will cost a significant amount of money. How will they get the amount they need?

BILLY KNOWS A SECRET

You keep secrets for a reason. It is usually to protect yourself or someone else. This story explores the issues of secret-keeping by Billy and Ant, and the consequences that arise. For children, the importance of finding a responsible adult with whom they can confide and share their concerns is a significant life lesson.

MULTIPLE FORMATS

Each of the Billy books is available as a **paperback**, as a **hardback** including coloured pictures, as **eBooks** and in **audio**-book format.

COLOURING BOOK

The Billy Colouring book is perfect for any budding artist to express themselves with fun and inspiring designs. Based on the Billy Series, it is filled with fan-favourite characters and has something for every Billy, Ant, Max and Jacko fan.

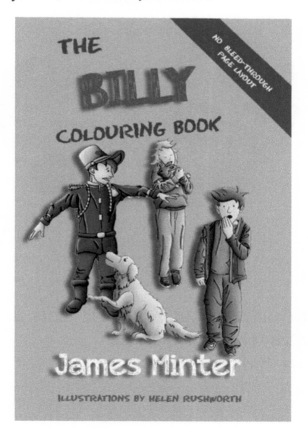

THE BILLY BOOK'S COLLECTIONS
VOLUMES 1 AND 2

For those readers who cannot wait for the
next book in the series, books 1, 2, 3, and 4
are combined into a single work — The
Billy Collection, Volume 1, whilst books 5,
6, 7, and 8 make up Volume 2.

The collections are still eligible for the free
activity books. Find them at
www.thebillybooks.co.uk .

ABOUT THE AUTHOR

I am a dad of two grown children and a stepfather to three more. I started writing five years ago with books designed to appeal to the inner child in adults - very English humour. My daughter Louise, reminded me of the bedtime stories I told her and suggested I write them down for others to enjoy. I haven't yet, but instead, I wrote this eight-book series for 7 to 9-year-old boys and girls. They are traditional stories dealing with negative behaviours with positive outcomes.

Although the main characters, Billy and his friends, are made up, Billy's dog, Jacko, is based on our much-loved family pet, which, with our second dog Malibu, caused havoc and mayhem to the delight of my children and consternation of me.

Prior to writing, I was a college lecturer and later worked in the computer industry, at a time before smartphones and tablets, when computers were powered by steam and stood as high as a bus.

WEBSITES

www.billygrowingup.com

www.thebillybooks.co.uk

www.jamesminter.com

E-MAIL

james@jamesminter.com

TWITTER

@james_minter

@thebillybooks

FACEBOOK

facebook.com/thebillybooks/

facebook.com/author.james.minter

ACKNOWLEDGEMENTS

Like all projects of this type, there are always a number of indispensable people who help bring it to completion. They include Christina Lepre, for her editing and incisive comments, suggestions and corrections. Harmony Kent for her proofreading, and Helen Rushworth of Ibex Illustrations, for her images that so capture the mood of the story. Gwen Gades for her cover design. And Maggie, my wife, for putting up with my endless pestering to read, comment and discuss my story, and, through her work as a personal development coach, her editorial input into the learnings designed to help children become responsible adults.

IBEX ILLUSTRATIONS